The Cat Who Decided

The almost true story of an Edinburgh cat

Margaret Forrester

Kelpies

Illustrated by Sandra Klaassen

Kelpies is an imprint of Floris Books

First published in 2007 by Floris Books
Second printing 2008
© 2007 Margaret Forrester

The publisher acknowledges a Lottery grant
from the Scottish Arts Council towards the
publication of this series.

British Library CIP Data available

ISBN 978-086315-531-4

Printed in Poland

For Catriona and Donald

Words marked like this* are explained in
the glossary.

Contents

1. Farm Kitten

Some time ago, on a farm near Edinburgh there was a farmyard cat. She worked hard to keep the rats away from the grain and all the food stored to feed the animals. The farmer was glad.

"Good old Puss," he said to the cat. "You help me a lot." And he scratched the cat's head. One cold January night, in a pile of straw in the old byre, the cat gave birth to four beautiful kittens. At least, three of them were beautiful.

The first was grey all over, except for a neat bib of white. He was handsome and looked like a bridegroom in a grey tailcoat.

"It would be nice to call him Bridegroom or Prince, but I expect he will be called Smokey," said the farmer's wife. "The postman wants a cat. I must remember to tell him when he comes with the letters tomorrow."

The second was golden with delicate russet stripes, like an autumn leaf.

"I think he should be called Maple," said the farmer's wife. "But I expect he will be called Marmalade or Ginger. The schoolteacher wants a cat. I must remember to tell her when I take her the sack of potatoes I promised."

The third was all black.

"I should like to call him Kiwi," said the farmer's wife, who had a vivid imagination and enjoyed giving her animals good names. "But I expect he will be called Sooty."

"Old Jock at the sheep farm up the hill wants a cat," said the farmer.

"Good," she replied, "I must remember to tell him when I see him at the market next week."

But the fourth kitten was a *mixter-maxter** sort of cat. He was black and dark brown and light brown. He had some stripes going one way and other stripes going another way. He had two white paws and two brown paws. The stripes on his face made a dark brown M on his forehead, and he had a bib of white fur under his chin and a white tummy.

"You're a mongrel moggie, if ever I saw one," said the farmer's wife. "What a brindled mixter-maxter cat you are! We'll have trouble finding a home for you.

Three people came to look at the kittens: the postman, the schoolteacher and Old Jock from the sheep farm up the hill.

The first cat was promised to the postman.

"Good! I always wanted a grey cat," said Postie, who wore a grey uniform himself. "When you come to live with me I shall call you Smokey."

The second cat was promised to the schoolteacher. "Good. I always wanted a ginger cat," said the schoolteacher, who had very ginger hair herself. "When you come to live with me I shall call you Ginger or maybe Marmalade."

The third cat was promised to Old Jock at the sheep farm up the hill.

"Good. I hope you are as good a mouser as your mother is," said Old Jock. "I have far too many rats in my barn." He looked at the all-black cat and then said with an air of discovery, "When you come to live with me I think I'll call you Sooty."

But nobody wanted the brindled mixter-maxter cat.

The farmer's wife put a post card in the window of the village shop. It read:

Free to good home

KITTEN

Will be excellent mouser

Apply to Robinsland Farm

But still nobody wanted the brindled mixter-maxter cat.

"Nobody loves me," he thought. "The others all have homes to go to."

The Postie came to the farm every day to deliver the mail. He always went to see Smokey and spent a long time talking to him and cuddling him while the farmer's wife looked at all the bills that had come in.

The schoolteacher brought all the children from the village school to see Ginger. They laughed when they heard that the kitten's name was Ginger, because privately they called the teacher

Ginger. They liked her very much and were glad that she had taken them to the farm to see her new kitten.

Old Jock made an excuse to visit every day, but everyone knew that it was to see Sooty. He brought little titbits of rabbit or chicken. Sooty was too young to eat food like that but his mother enjoyed it while Old Jock gave Sooty a tickle under the chin.

"Everyone has a visitor except me," thought the brindled mixter-maxter cat. He began to feel very lonely and sad.

"Never mind," said the farmer's wife, who had taken a liking to this funny looking kitten. "Something will turn up. Remember, looks are not everything." And she picked up the little kitten and stroked him.

"But it's nice to be pretty," said her daughter, who was at the age when these things matter.

"Handsome is as handsome does," said her mother enigmatically. "Mark my words, that cat has character. He will go far." But she sighed all the same.

2. Journeying Cat

Nobody wanted the brindled mixter-maxter kitten. He did not feed well and he was sad.

"Nobody loves me," he thought. "The others all have homes to go to. Everyone has a visitor except me. Maybe I shall decide to go away. Perhaps I could find a home for myself. But I don't know how. Besides, I'm scared."

When the kittens were eight weeks old they went to their new homes. Only the brindled mixter-maxter kitten was left.

The farmer's wife said, "He is not doing well. Nobody wants him."

Then her daughter who worked in an office in the city said, "We have mice in the office. Perhaps a cat would keep them away. I'll take the kitten there."

Everyone cheered up. It seemed to be a good solution. So the brindled mixter-maxter kitten was put into a cardboard box, lined with plastic and newspaper, ("in case of accidents," said the farmer's wife) and travelled with the farmer's daughter to Edinburgh.

On the journey to the city, the kitten was very frightened. The bus jerked and bumped when it moved, and made a roaring noise. He slipped around inside the cardboard box. "I don't like this one little bit," he thought. "I hope we get there soon."

When the bus stopped, the farmer's daughter walked from the bus stop to the office, carrying the kitten in the cardboard box. People hurried past them, anxious to get to work on time. The mixter-maxter kitten was still frightened because the box was dark and there were strange smells and noises all around him. He wanted to be back on the farm.

When the farmer's daughter arrived in the office with the cardboard box, everyone crowded around to see. They laughed when they saw him.

"What a funny looking cat."

"What a mixter-maxter kitten."

"We shall have to call him Tartan."

"That's not my name," thought the brindled mixter-maxter kitten.

"Or Motley."

"That's not my name either," said the kitten to himself.

For three miserable days and nights the brindled mixter-maxter kitten lived in the office. The days were noisy and busy and frightening. Sometimes the typists would give him a little milk in a saucer or some biscuit crumbs. But they were too busy to see that he was lonely and not eating. The nights were quiet and lonely and frightening. There were strange noises of emptiness in the vast building. Sometimes the mice came out and laughed at him.

"I've been here long enough," he said. "I want to go home. Back to the farm."

Three days later the head of department came into the office. He was a big man with large hands, a red florid complexion and a very loud voice.

"Here comes the Boss," the staff said in low voices.

The Boss looked round the office and then spotted the mixter-maxter kitten.

"Bless me," he said, "what on earth is that cat doing here? Animals are not allowed." He began to frown and look angry. Just then three things happened.

The brindled mixter-maxter kitten yawned enormously, for the mice had kept him awake all night. He looked so sweet with his shell pink tongue and pearl white teeth that the Boss looked again.

Then the brindled mixter-maxter kitten miaowed in a high-pitched little voice, because the staff had forgotten to feed him and he was *so* hungry.

Then the brindled mixter-maxter kitten decided he liked the Boss with his large hands and his red florid complexion and loud voice, so he took a few unsteady steps forward until he reached the Boss's large shiny brown shoes.

The Boss smiled all over his red florid face. "My wife would know what to do with you," he said. To the staff he said, "I shall take him home with me at the end of the day." And he did.

The Boss lined the cardboard box with paper and plastic in case of accidents and put in his own tartan wool scarf. With his great big hands he tickled the brindled mixter-maxter kitten under his chin. "We'll soon sort you out," he said. "You'll be happy at Number Five."

But the brindled mixter-maxter kitten was not so sure. "I shall wait and see," he thought.

At the end of the day, the Boss packed his brief case with work to do at home, and put on his coat and hat and gloves. He spent a long time looking for his tartan scarf before he remembered that it was in the box with the kitten. Then balancing the box carefully with all his books and papers, he walked to the car park, opened the door of the car and put the box with the brindled mixter-maxter kitten on the back seat.

The car was nearly as noisy as the bus and there was still a great roar of traffic. The kitten crouched in the box and tried to see out through the little holes that the Boss had made. But all he could see was the inside of the car.

Suddenly all was quiet and dark. They had reached the Boss's house and parked in the garage. The Boss climbed out of the car and balancing the box with the brindled mixter-maxter kitten in it, he collected everything else, walked through the garden and opened the back door. "That's it for the day. Home, sweet home!" he said.

But the brindled mixter-maxter kitten was not so sure. "I shall wait and see," he thought.

3. The House at Number Five

Number Five turned out to be a tall thin house in a long row of joined up houses. "Alice!" shouted the Boss. "Come and see what I brought you today!" And he told her the whole story.

The Boss's wife was an artist. She was called Alice. She did not really want a kitten because she was so busy painting. But when she opened the cardboard box, she said, "What an adorable kitten, Fred. How pretty he is." She picked him up. "You have a beautiful M on your forehead. That means you are a tabby cat."

Then she noticed how weak and wobbly he was. "Gracious me," she said, and her eyes flashed with anger. "They have not looked after him properly." The mixter-maxter kitten was too weak to eat, too wobbly to stand. He wanted his mummy and he was sad.

"We'll soon sort you out," said Alice. First she made a cosy bed for him in the kitchen. She used the same cardboard box so that he could still have the comforting farm smells. But she made it soft and warm and secure. Then she telephoned the vet and asked for advice. She warmed up some special milk and put it drop by drop into the mixter-maxter kitten's mouth.

Every two hours she fed the mixter-maxter kitten. She even got up in the middle of the night to feed him and she kept the kitchen warm for them both. She began to like the mixter-maxter kitten.

"You have spirit," she said.

"Have I?" wondered the kitten. "Is that a good thing to have?" He began to feel better.

On Monday he was able to lick the milk out of a saucer.

On Tuesday he had some chicken broth.

On Wednesday he had some fish mashed with milk.

And on Thursday he had a spoonful of chopped up chicken.

The mixter-maxter kitten began to feel much better. He stretched himself and began to take his first careful steps around the kitchen. Alice picked him up and tickled him behind his ear. "We've made it," she said, and smiled at him. And the mixter-maxter kitten purred his thanks and his happiness.

"You look a very Scottish cat," said Alice. "I wonder what your name is?" And the mixter-maxter kitten purred louder than ever. No one had asked him before. "I think you look like a Mac," said Alice. And Mac thought he would burst with the joy of his purring because she had discovered his name.

Mac liked Alice very much. He wanted to be with her always. But Alice was a painter and she did not let him come into her studio when she painted pictures. The studio smelt of turpentine and oil. It was a strong smell. Mac twitched his nose.

"No, my friend," said Alice, "I can't let you come in. You would jump on my canvases and play with my brushes and you would get paint on your beautiful fur."

Mac thought that if he tried hard, he could stay very still, but Alice was stern about this.

"Paint and cats don't mix," she said. "Unless you are Elizabeth Blackadder," she added, a little wistfully. So however hard Mac miaowed, he was never allowed inside the studio with its strange strong smells.

Mac decided he would make do with the big front room. Sometimes he slept on the sofa. Sometimes he sat on the table in the bay window and watched people passing. And because there was no one there to look after him, he did all sorts of things that were clever but just a little naughty.

One day he explored the curtains in the front room. They were very grand lined curtains of faded brocade. Because the curtains had been hanging in the room for at least forty years, the linings were soft and torn. One day, Mac discovered that if he climbed up the curtains on the inside, he could slip through a rip inside the lining. To begin with it was fun to swing in the curtain like children in the swing park. But when he tried to get out he discovered he couldn't!

"Help!" he miaowed in his high-pitched voice. "Help! Come and rescue me and I shall never be naughty again."

But nobody heard him. So he curled up inside the gently swaying curtain and fell fast asleep. That evening Alice and Fred came into the front room and called and called.

"Mac! Where are you?" But there was no reply. They searched everywhere before sitting down to have a late supper watching television in the front room.

"Don't worry, Alice," said Fred, "He'll turn up." He walked to the windows. "It's getting dark," he said. "I'll just draw the curtains." But as he started to move the curtain he could feel something different about it. "Bless me, there's something inside the curtain." The small bulge in the curtain woke up.

"It's me," miaowed Mac. "I just wanted to play. And now I am *so* hungry I could eat an elephant!" When he was lifted out he scampered through to the kitchen to have his supper.

Best of all Mac liked to be out in the garden. It was only a small garden and most of it was taken up with a garage, but there were flowers and some grass and the earth smelt nearly as good as the farmyard. Mac was happy enough, but he wanted someone to be his special friend.

Sometimes, when Alice was working, she forgot the time and Mac would begin to feel hungry. It was then he discovered the world beyond the House at Number Five.

4. Mac, Explorer

One day, when Mac was feeling both brave and hungry, he decided to be an explorer. First he explored every corner of the kitchen, but there were only the porridge plates left over from breakfast. He decided he would give them a quick clean to help Alice. In the front room, he found a silver chocolate wrapper scrunched up in the waste paper basket. The only way he could reach it was by climbing to the rim of the basket. When he reached the rim, the whole basket fell over. Mac was surprised, but soon realized that by walking inside the basket he could get it to roll over and over. It was good fun and he did it until he was tired of that game. Then he remembered about the chocolate wrapper. There was no chocolate in it. But he played at football with the silver paper ball for a little time. He found some cheese crumbs on the hearth rug and they tasted good.

The linings of the curtains had been stitched up so he couldn't do much there. But as he looked at the old curtains hanging from a great height he suddenly knew that he wanted to sit at the top of them, right up on the pelmet. He launched himself at the curtains and reached half way up before his strength gave out and he had to jump down. He tried it a few times more, and then had the brilliant idea of trying the jump from higher up. What better launchpad than the grand piano which stood close by? He scrambled onto the piano stool and then on to the keys. They made an extraordinary noise. He forgot about climbing the curtains and ran up and down the keys with delight. Then he discovered something even more interesting. The piano was open and there were things inside. Firmly he stepped onto the strings and was rewarded with such a lovely noisy twang! A door banged in the house.

"Better disappear," he thought and scampered into the kitchen. "I think I shall explore the garden." The kitchen window had been left open just a crack. It was big enough for him to slide through if he made himself go very flat.

Outside in the garden, Mac looked at the bluebells and the ferns. The sun shone warm on his back. And he suddenly felt very brave. "That iron railing has plenty of room for someone my size," he thought. "I shall just slip through and visit the garden next door." And he did.

It was a lovely garden. There were lots of plants in it but it was also wild and there were many places where he could hide. There was no garage at the foot of that garden — just two lovely trees. One was a lilac tree and it was in full blossom.

"I know how to climb that," thought Mac. And without thinking he scrambled up the wide trunk, clinging to the bark with his sharp little claws. Soon he was walking along the low bough that gave such a good view of the garden. He sat carefully in the middle of the bough and thought about himself.

"How did I manage to do that?" he thought. "No one ever taught me to climb a tree. I just looked at it and knew that I could do it. And this feels a lot better than climbing curtains. Perhaps cats are made for climbing trees. Perhaps trees are made for cats to climb." He sat in the spring sunshine and thought about the situation. Then he gave himself a lick all over. "When in doubt," his mother had told him, "when in doubt, wash. It gives you time to think." So Mac licked himself carefully all over. It was a good feeling. He sat and looked out at the view.

The garden was beautiful. There was so much more of it than in his place. There were tall stately tulips of very pale pink and others of midnight purple. There were drifts of purple aubrietia and chalk white candytuft. There were lots of plants growing in the warm spring sunshine. There was a grass lawn. The earth smelled so good and full of life — it reminded him of the farm.

Mac scrambled down the tree and walked carefully around the tulips. He nibbled at the young grass. He sniffed at the catmint leaves just beginning to unfurl. He jumped onto the wooden garden seat and sat on the flat arm. The sun felt warm on his fur and the warmth soaked through to his bones. He closed his eyes and opened them again, narrow ovals of topaz. He looked over the railing at the tall thin house that belonged to him and Fred and Alice. And he looked up at the tall thin house in front of him that belonged to other people.

"I should like to meet them," he said to himself. "If I can climb a tree," he thought, "maybe I can open doors too." Suddenly he realized that he was very hungry. "Perhaps the other people, whoever they are, will give me something to eat." And he walked purposefully towards their back door.

5. The House Next Door

When he reached the back door, he found that it had been wedged open to let in the warm spring air. Mac stepped delicately over the threshold.

"I am an explorer," he thought. He twitched his nose. The kitchen was the same size as his own but it looked and smelt different. Gently he padded through the hall and up the staircase. "I shall introduce myself," thought Mac. "The back door is open. If I am not welcome, I can escape very easily."

So he walked into the upstairs drawing room where two elderly ladies were having afternoon tea. There was a low round table with a tray at the bay window. On the tray there were cups with roses on them and a big fat silver teapot. The two women were nibbling sponge cake and sipping tea from the cups decorated with roses. Mac looked for a long time before deciding to introduce himself. He miaowed, quite loudly for a cat that was only five months old.

"Helen! What on earth is that?" said one of the women.

"Why it's Mac from next door," said the woman called Helen. "He has come to pay us a visit. Oh I am glad. Emily, can we give him something to eat or drink?"

"They know my name," thought Mac, and he purred in the most encouraging way. They poured some milk into a saucer and Mac, who was not overly fond of milk, drank politely, carefully keeping an eye on them and the open door.

"I think we should buy some cat food the next time we go shopping," said Emily. "Then we can be sure of having something tasty for him when he comes to visit."

"That sounds good," thought Mac, and he purred gently, by way of encouragement. He shook himself politely when the milk was finished, washed his whiskers carefully, circled the whole room and then slipped out of the door, down the stairs and out into the garden.

"I've done it," he said. "I have found another home. When Alice is too busy to feed me, the two ladies will let me come in and I can have something to eat with them. Good. Now I have two homes."

For the rest of that first year, Mac enjoyed his two homes. Mostly he was with Alice and Fred. But when Alice was busy or when Alice and Fred went away for the weekend, Mac would visit the house next door and sleep on the best cushions in the front room. He loved the two ladies' garden very much.

He climbed the lilac tree every day and sharpened his growing claws on its trunk. He loved to lie on the wide low branch and view the world. Spring turned to summer and Mac played with the butterflies in the garden. Summer turned to autumn and Mac danced with the falling leaves. Autumn turned to winter and the gardens went to sleep. Sometimes Mac sat on the table in the bay window of the front room at Number Five and watched the rain falling like needles.

"I am glad that I have decided to stay inside today," he would say.

And sometimes if he wanted company, he went to the house next door and was given crunchy cat treats and cool creamy milk. Mac had the best of both worlds.

So Mac began to forget the farmyard, except sometimes in his dreams. As the year passed he grew very beautiful. The fur on his coat was mahogany brown. His stripes grew to be regular and even. His white and brown socks were elegant and distinctive. His bib was thick and soft and fluffy. But best of all his whiskers became extremely long and pure white. People stopped in the street when he sat at the window.

"What an elegant cat!" they would say.

Not only was he elegant, he also became big and strong. There were other cats in the neighbourhood and sometimes when Alice and Fred were asleep, Mac ventured far beyond his own two gardens. There were several secret fights on those nights, fights that no one observed, although some light sleepers heard them in the distance. Sometimes Mac limped home with a few scratches on his head and a sore paw. He would stay at home for several days after that, licking the sore places, resting and eating voraciously. Once, Alice and Fred had to take him to the vet with a torn ear.

"He'll survive," said the vet. "He's a bit of a bruiser this one. Likes fighting does he?"

Alice was horrified. "Certainly not. He never fights."

The vet grinned. He had heard that story before.
"Most cats have two sides to them," he said. "He
may be soft and sweet to you, but mark my words,
that cat is a bonnie *fechter**!" And he stroked Mac.
He liked a cat with character.

6. Christmas is Coming

Just as Mac was feeling settled and comfortable and sure of himself, something new happened. One day, Alice packed away her canvases. She cleaned all her paintbrushes. She closed the studio door. "It will soon be Christmas," she said, "I must begin to get ready."

The tall thin house had three floors with lots of stairs. Most of the rooms were closed. But now, Alice went up to the top of the house and opened each door. She opened the window in every room, even although it was chilly.

"We shall let some air in," she said. "The children are coming home for Christmas."

"Children?" said Mac, "Children? No one told me about children. I shall have to think about this." And he followed her up the stairs to see what she was going to do.

The girls' room had twin beds. The walls had old posters of pop stars and film stars. There were hockey sticks and tennis rackets in the corner. Old dolls lined the mantelpiece. A whole family of bears sat on the window seat. The bookcase had battered volumes with names like, *French Grammar, The Elements of Trigonometry, Lamb's Tales from Shakespeare,* and a pile of very old *School Friend* annuals.

The wardrobe was stuffed full of old blazers and pinafores, party dresses and one long bridesmaid's dress. The chest of drawers was full of old jerseys and scarves and gloves with holes in them. Alice closed the drawers quickly. She did not really like housework.

"I shall clean this out so that Jenny and her husband John can sleep here," said Alice. She cleaned the room from top to bottom. She put crisp white sheets on each bed and made them up with blankets, old-fashioned counterpanes and quilts covered in a soft rose coloured slippery satin. She laid out clean pink towels and fresh soap. She put some ivy and Christmas roses in a crystal vase. Mac looked at the beds and the soft quilts with longing and he sighed because he knew better than to have a nap there. Besides, he wanted to know what would happen in the next room.

"That looks better, Mac," Alice said, as she surveyed the room. Mac said nothing. He was not sure about Christmas and children.

The boys' room also had two beds. The walls had posters of rugby players and the very first aeroplanes. There were ancient golf clubs and a tennis racquet with broken strings in one corner. Model ships and planes lined the mantelpiece. Boxes of games were on the window seat — games like chess and draughts, Meccano and Subbuteo. The bookcase had piles of old comics in it and books with titles like *Coral Island, An Approach to Latin Grammar, (part 1), Elementary Calculus,* and *Biggles Fails to Return.*

The wardrobe was stuffed full of old blazers and grey flannel trousers, torn jeans, rugby shirts and tweed jackets with leather patches on the elbows.

The chest of drawers was full of old jerseys and scarves and socks that didn't match. Alice closed the drawers quickly. She did not really like housework.

"I shall clean this out so that Colin and his partner Sybil can sleep here," said Alice. She cleaned the room from top to bottom. She put crisp white sheets on the beds and made them up with blankets, old-fashioned counterpanes and quilts covered in fern green silk. She laid out clean green towels and fresh soap. She put some holly and winter jasmine in a Chinese bowl.

"That looks better, Mac," she said. Mac said nothing. He was not sure about Christmas and children.

The third room had a single bed in it. It was the guest room. The wardrobe was empty. The chest of drawers was empty. The mantelpiece had some pretty but dusty ornaments on it. The window seat had some plump brightly coloured cushions. The bookcase was full of titles like, *The Makings of Classical Edinburgh, The Silent Traveller in Edinburgh, Memoirs of a Highland Lady, Cockburn's Memorials* and *A Scots Quair.*

"I shall clean this out so that Paddy can sleep here when he gets back from Paris," said Alice. She cleaned the room from top to bottom. She put crisp white sheets on the bed and made it up with blankets, a quilt with a blue and orange Paisley pattern and a pale blue candlewick cover that had tufts missing. She laid out clean blue towels and fresh soap. She put some rosemary and pearly white honesty into a tall thin pottery jug. This time she sighed a little. "Everything looks so old-fashioned. We should move to a smaller house and get rid of half this old stuff. But I don't think I have the energy."

"What?" thought Mac, "Move? I'm not going anywhere."

"Anyway," Alice went on, "Fred doesn't want to move." And she pulled the bedcover straight.

"That looks better, Mac," she said.

Mac said nothing. He was not sure about Christmas and children.

"Just as well that Bronwen can't come too," said Alice, "She's got herself a job in London over Christmas. That will help to pay her through Drama College." And she smiled at Mac. She was glad that three of her four children were coming home.

Mac said nothing. He still was not sure about Christmas and children.

7. The Grown-up Children

Alice spent the next few days making lists and going shopping, then cooking and baking. Ham simmered on the hob beside pots of soup and more soup. Nuts were toasted, cream was whipped, egg whites were beaten, and vegetables were scrubbed and peeled. Such lovely smells! Ginger and cinnamon, oranges and lemons, sponges and biscuits, pies and cakes — the warm, sweet, spicy flavours and fragrances filled the air.

Fred spent the evenings putting up a long green outdoor thing in the bay window where Mac liked to sit. It was a tree!

"Good!" thought Mac. "Now I won't have to go outside in the cold to scratch my claws." But it was not for him. Soon silly little electric lights shone on the tree and Mac was not allowed near.

"I don't like Christmas in the front room," thought Mac. "It is better in the kitchen." So he stayed close to Alice and the lovely tantalizing smells.

"The children will arrive soon," said Alice, "I just have time to make a batch of scones."

All of a sudden, the world changed for Mac. The doorbell rang noisily. The first two children surged into the house. But these were not children — he had seen children at the farm. They were grown-up.

They were called Jenny and John and they came from London. Alice and Fred, Jenny and

John — that made four grown-ups. Later, Colin and Sybil came from Cornwall. That made six grown-ups. Very much later Paddy flew in from Paris. And all seven grown-ups talked loudly all the time. They filled the house and banged doors and laughed. They ate lots of food — they loved Alice's soup and scones and laughed even more when they saw the gingerbread animals.

"Just like when we were children," they said.

"I thought they *were* children," puzzled Mac.

They drank port and ate *Dunsyre Blue** cheese. "Can't get this where we live," they said. They slept late and made coffee at strange times.

Alice and Fred loved it and talked about what fun it was to have the children home.

"But they aren't children," thought Mac. "I don't like grown-up children."

On Christmas Day, they all went to church.

"What a relief," thought Mac.

Not only was the house quiet and empty, but there were the most wonderful smells coming from the kitchen and wafting around the entire house.

Mac prowled around and sniffed appreciatively. "Alice will give me some of that," he thought, "I shall just go and check the dining room."

On the table there were silver candlesticks with shiny red candles. There was a trail of winter jasmine and tiny ivy leaves wreathed around each candlestick. Polished silver cutlery gleamed on the table. The best crystal wine glasses sparkled at each place. A cold ham studded with cloves sat on the sideboard next to a huge trifle trembling with good things. At every place there was a plate of

the best china. On each plate there were curls of
smoked salmon, triangles of thin brown bread and
thick wedges of lemon.

Mac jumped onto a chair and then very delicately stepped on to the table, his whiskers quiver-
ing with delight. He knew better than to nibble the
salmon, no matter how tempted he felt. But the
lordly dishes of fresh butter suddenly reminded
him of the dairy on the farmyard so long ago.

"Just one lick won't matter," he thought. It

tasted good. "The butter looks different now," he thought. "I better make the other one look the same." And he licked the second dish of butter with his rough feline tongue. That tasted good too.

As he heard the key turn in the lock of the front door, he jumped lightly from table to floor and glided silently from the dining room to the kitchen.

They all had a wonderful Christmas dinner. It

lasted from one o'clock until half past four. Mac
had smoked salmon *and* turkey *and* ham.

"Mum," said Jenny, "You really are amazing.
Everything was perfect. And such attention to
detail. You even put a pattern on the butter!"

"Nothing too good for you children," said Alice.
But she looked sharply at the butter and then at
Mac, who ever so slowly, closed his eyes and turned
his head away. "Mac and I did it together," she
said, and smiled to herself as the grown-up children clattered into the kitchen and began to wash
up.

8. A New Friend

It was lunchtime on Boxing Day. At least it was for Fred and Alice. They had wakened early, had breakfast at the usual time, then they went out for a walk by the sea at Cramond. For lunch they had cream of leek soup followed by cold ham and spiced apple chutney. Then they sat by the fire with Mac and did a Christmas crossword together. But the five grown-up children all did their own thing. Jenny and John got up at ten o'clock, took toast and tea and went out to climb Blackford Hill. Colin and Sybil came down at eleven o'clock, made black coffee, spoke in soft voices and went back to bed. Paddy came down at one o'clock, and opened the fridge. He helped himself to a huge plate of left over trifle, a mince pie, a wedge of cheese and a tumbler of orange juice. He switched on the television and filled the room with noise.

"This is brilliant, Mum," he said, "It's the best Christmas I've had for years. If only Bronwen were here, it would be perfect."

"In a way, it's just as well," said Alice. "Her room is filled with all the junk in the house and Mac's the only one who is sleeping there just now."

Jenny and John came back from their walk. They heated up some soup, filled their plates with food, joined in the crossword and looked at television at the same time. Colin and Sybil decided they couldn't get back to sleep. So they came downstairs and joined in the fun.

Just then the doorbell rang. On the doorstep
was a very thin girl in jeans with a long striped
scarf and an enormous backpack. She had short
dark hair and big brown eyes.

"Hi Mum and Dad," she said, "Is there any food?
I'm starving."

"Bronwen!" everyone shouted.

"I've been given a few days off," she explained.
"I was offered a lift. We've been travelling since
four o'clock this morning." After something to eat,
Bronwen wanted to sleep.

"I'm sorry, darling," said Alice, "it may be a little
crowded in your room, and the radiator is broken.
But I have put a hot water bottle in your bed."

"Doesn't matter," yawned Bronwen, "I'm so
tired, I could sleep anywhere."

To reach her room, she had to walk through the
kitchen, into the scullery, and up a narrow stair,
which led only to one room.

The room was full of things that were going to be
mended later or being kept just in case. There were
stepladders, broken easels, boxes of books for the
annual book sale at St Andrew's and St George's
Church in George Street. There were cushions
waiting to be re-covered, a satinwood table with a
broken leg, a small rosewood rocking chair with a
torn cane seat and a box of dried up looking dahlia
tubers. There was a quarter violin with a broken
bow. There were old ice skates, some golf clubs and
plastic sacks full of old curtains and clothes. There
was a box marked "Great Aunt Elizabeth's Silver
Tea Set," a big basket full of wool and odds and
ends of tapestries and knitting, a Singer sewing

machine with a hand-operated wheel, and cartons of sheet music.

And there, tucked into a corner below the eaves, was a bed. Bronwen kicked off her boots, pulled off her jeans and slid under the old cotton quilt with the pattern of faded roses. She shivered at first and her breath came out like clouds in the sharp cold air.

Just as she was dropping off to sleep, the door was slowly pushed open and Mac insinuated himself into the room.

"Wow," said Bronwen, "So you're Mac — the new puss cat. I've heard of you. I'm sorry if I have taken your bed. You're welcome to share."

Mac stood on his hind legs, with his front paws leaning on the old bed. He looked at the comfortable hump under the quilt. Very gently, he slid his head and front paws under the covers and climbed in. Bronwen touched the soft thick fur and stroked him slowly from head to tail.

"Sorry we have to share, Mac. We shall just have to keep each other warm." And the little bed throbbed to the sound of Mac's purring as they slept together that cold Boxing Day.

Mac enjoyed his first Christmas. There were good things to eat. Whether the grown-up children were eating or drinking, or talking, or watching television, or singing round the piano, or playing games, one of them would be sure to scoop up Mac and give him a cuddle. In the evenings, Mac chose which lap to sit on, but usually he chose Bronwen.

"Bronwen," he thought, "is my special friend."

9. The Musical Doctors

The noisy Christmas passed and the children who were grown-up went away. The house returned to its usual quiet.

Spring came again and Mac enjoyed going outside. He liked the garden of Number Seven so much better than the one in Number Five. He loved the two beautiful trees. The taller of the two was an ash tree and Mac sometimes climbed to the very top. But it was so very tall that it made him feel too far away. Besides, some noisy grey squirrels lived there. He realized instinctively that there has to be room for everyone in the garden so he politely did not bother them often. Besides, he preferred the lilac tree. Whether it was flowering in spring, leafy in summer, golden in autumn, or bare and leafless in the winter snow, Mac loved to lie on the wide low branch and view the garden. In January the yellow aconites with their green ruffled collars grew in the thick leaf mould. In February the fat shiny snowdrops danced beneath the witch hazel. After that, daffodils blew in the fierce March winds. When summer came the garden was filled with all sorts of colours and intoxicating smells and sounds. Best of all were great clumps of catmint and Mac rolled over and over on them.

Mac also loved to visit the two gentle sisters who lived in Number Seven. There was something very special about Dr Helen and Dr Emily. They were not doctors of medicine. They made music. They were

musical doctors. Dr Emily played the violin and Dr
Helen played the cello. Mac loved to hear them play.
Sometimes he would slip in to Number Seven. He
liked the cello best and would pad delicately into Dr
Helen's room and gently push open the door. She
often played with her eyes closed because she felt
the music so deeply. So Mac listened with his head

in the air and his eyes closed too. When she had finished he sat up straight and tall and purred loudly.

"So," she smiled, "you like Bach, do you?"

Dr Helen and Dr Emily taught music to many boys and girls. They believed that every child could love and play music. Often groups of children came to their house to practise their cello or violin. Sometimes it sounded quite nice and Mac listened with his head in the air. "That's quite good," he would say. And Dr Helen and Dr Emily would clap their hands and tell the children how good they were. They gave the children home-made sponge cake and ginger snaps. The children really liked that. It made them want to practise harder for next time.

Sometimes the noise was dreadful. When that happened, Mac flattened his ears against his head.

"I can make a noise like that," said Mac. And he would leave the room with his tail in the air. Dr Helen and Dr Emily knew that when Mac left the room it was time for everyone to have a rest and the two doctors fed the children on home-made shortbread and cherry cake. The children really liked that too. They promised to practise harder for next time.

When the last children had gone, clutching their music cases and their school bags and all their paraphernalia, Mac would quietly pad up to the drawing room where the two musical doctors sipped their tea from the cups with roses.

After tea, Helen practised for recitals that she gave with her sister. She played many pieces of music. But there were some that Mac loved very much indeed. When she played those, Mac would lift up his head and purr.

"So," she would say, "you really *do* like Bach best, you clever cat."

The only thing that Mac did *not* like about the musical doctors was that they were so busy making music they rarely came into the garden. They never weeded or pruned or hoed or dug or raked. So they decided to engage a gardener who came once a fortnight in the summer to care for the garden.

Now the gardener hated cats. He thought they were as bad as snails and slugs and squirrels for spoiling the garden. The first time the gardener came Mac approached politely to say "Hello" and "Welcome to my garden." He walked down the path that wound between the catmint on one side and on the other side the pink flowers that are called *London Pride* in England and *Nancy Pretty* in Scotland. His whiskers were smiling in pleasure and his tail was waving above his back, full of confidence. If Mac had been vain he would have known what a beautiful picture he made. As it was, he was simply friendly and interested.

"Cats!" muttered the gardener. "Cats are pests. Cats are trouble. I hate cats." And he picked up his ball of twine and flung it at Mac. Mac was outraged. The twine had not hit him but he knew that the gardener was An Enemy. He sprinted to the back of the garden and scrambled up the lilac tree, peeping out from the leafy branches.

The ball of twine unravelled as the gardener threw it and now he wound it up again, muttering the while. From then on, Mac enjoyed the garden most days, but when the gardener came, Mac disappeared back to Number Five.

10. Gold Watch Time

That second year, Mac was no longer a kitten. He was fully grown. As well as being big and strong, he was very beautiful and he was loving and warm. But sometimes he was lonely. He wanted someone to choose *him*. He longed for someone to love *him*. He longed for someone that *he* could love with all his heart.

* The farmer's wife had not wanted him.
* No one in the village had chosen him.
* The girls in the office had only wanted him to catch mice.
* Alice had been good to him but she often forgot about him.
* Bronwen had loved him for a whole week and then had gone back to London.
* Dr Helen and Dr Emily liked him but did they want him to live there? They were always so taken up with their music pupils.
* And they had a nasty gardener who didn't like cats.

Mac wondered about all these things. He really wanted a family who would love him and play with him and feed him well. In return he would look after them and stay with them always. How he wished that he had a family that had chosen him and not just been sorry for him. And he sighed, puzzled by so many things in his life.

One day Fred came home and said, "Guess what? Gold Watch time is coming sooner than I expected!" He told Alice that his office was to be reorganized. All the staff were being moved. "So I can take early retirement," he said. "It's what we had hoped would happen. Now we can go and visit the family and perhaps settle in France near to Paddy."

"Painting in France!" said Alice. "It would be an artist's dream." And she started to imagine the Left Bank in Paris or a country cottage in Provence.

"There will be parties and farewells first," said Fred. "The Department is going to give me a big dinner party!" And he wondered what he would buy with the money they would give him — maybe a new car!

For the occasion, Fred put on his dinner jacket and bow tie. Alice put on her best black velvet dress, her long pearls and her crimson shawl with the deep fringe. She swept up her unruly hair with a tortoiseshell comb. There was a delicious dinner with wine and lots of speeches. They gave Alice a big bouquet of flowers. They gave Fred a gold watch and an envelope with a cheque in it. It was a happy sad time for Fred.

The next day the office staff gave another party. They had tea and a home made cake and sparkling wine. They gave Alice more flowers. They gave Fred a book token and a great big cheer. "He was a good boss," they said to each other. "He was always fair."

Mac did not realize at first how much things

would change. "I managed Christmas and the Grown-up Children," he thought, "I managed to find a second home and a better garden. Surely I can manage Gold Watch Time too."

Fred could not settle to retirement. He moved restlessly around the house all day. He interrupted Alice in the studio. He wanted to drink cups of tea or coffee with her. He wanted to go out for walks together.

Alice sighed. "I just want to finish this painting for the exhibition," she said. "Go for a walk on your own."

Still Fred could not settle. He felt he had nothing to do. All his friends were still working. He wasn't any good at golf. He didn't like bowling. He wasn't good at painting. He didn't want to go for walks on his own.

They started to talk seriously of buying another home nearer to the grown-up children in the south of England, or even going to live in France for good. Alice wasn't so sure but she knew that something had to change.

"All right," she said. "All right. Why not? Yes. Let's look at France properly. The light in Provence is wonderful for painting. Let's go there and have a scout around."

"Good idea," said Fred. "This weather is blooming depressing." And he looked out of the window at the rain falling. "It's only September," he said, "we should be getting better weather than this. There will be snow on the Pentlands next!"

"Where is France?" thought Mac. "I hope it isn't too far away."

Mac was glad that he already had a second home. Maybe it was time for him to move house. "I shall wait and see," he thought. "But I shall decide what is good for me, no one else!"

11. "I Hate Changes!"

That autumn things happened very quickly.

"I hate changes!" said Mac.

Fred and Alice became very excited at the thought of moving nearer to their family, and especially at the thought of living in France. They decided to take the car and drive south visiting the grown-up children in England and then on to Paris to see Paddy. After that they would travel around France and look at houses to rent or buy. The plan was to be away for several months. They would spend Christmas down south with the family.

"You can't spend Christmas away! What about the silver and the china and the turkey and the ham and the cooking? What about my Christmas dinner?" said Mac. "What about Bronwen? I hate changes!"

Alice and Fred took out the suitcases and bags that had been stored in the back room where Mac slept and where he and Bronwen had kept each other warm at Christmas time. Mac walked round and round the suitcases as Fred and Alice tried to pack.

"Should I go with them?" he thought. But he decided that France was very far away. So he circled around the suitcases and then slipped off to see Dr Helen and Dr Emily.

"What about Mac?" said Alice, "We can't just leave him."

"Come on, Alice," said Fred, "He's only a cat! Someone will look after him. Why not ask Helen and Emily?"

"Well," said Alice doubtfully, "I'm not sure that they are up to it. Emily is beginning to look quite frail. Perhaps we should find another home for him. I'll ask around."

Alice and Fred would not have left Mac without someone to take care of him. They knew that he had made friends with the gentle sisters next door and so they were the first people to ask. Helen and Emily were delighted. It was arranged that Mac would live with them while Alice and Fred were away.

"Of course we shall look after Mac," they said. "He will be no trouble."

"But do they really *want* me?" said Mac. "Or are they just being kind? And what about the nasty gardener?"

"What I really want," he thought, "is a family who will not move. A family with nice children, like Bronwen, only younger, who will stay in the house and let me do what I want and will love me because I am me, myself, Mac."

The more he thought about it, the more he thought it was important for *him* to choose and not just to let other people choose for him.

"Yes," he thought, "I want to find a family who will love me because I am me, myself, Mac. Not because I can catch mice or because they are sorry for me or because they are being kind to their neighbours but because they really, really want me myself, Mac."

He remembered how the farmer's wife had written out a card to put in the shop window and it had read:

> Free to good home
>
> KITTEN
>
> Will be excellent mouser
>
> Apply to Robinsland Farm

"Perhaps," he thought, "if I knew how to spell, I could write a card for a shop." And he decided that the card would say:

> WANTED!
>
> Good family with kind children
>
> Who will love Mac
>
> Because he is Mac
>
> Apply to Mac at number five

Mac watched as Alice and Fred chose which suitcases and maps, which easels and brushes, which picnic baskets and travelling rugs were to go with them. He watched as they took out walking boots

and sticks, cameras and binoculars from the cupboard in the hall. They packed summer clothes as
well as winter woollies. They packed swimsuits
and waterproofs. They packed sandals and sun
hats.

Alice and Fred went to the house next door to
make final arrangements about Mac. "We shall
take several months for our trip," said Alice. "Are
you sure that it is all right to look after Mac for so
long? We shall take him back when we return. If
by any chance we find our dream house in France
or England we shall let you know so that we can
discuss Mac's future."

"We'll see about that," thought Mac. "I am not
a sack of potatoes to be given from one person to
another. I am not a parcel to be handed between
families as though I have no feelings. I shall decide
where to stay. I shall think about it and then find
a family who will stay in one place and not move
me around." He went into the garden and wandered among the dahlias and chrysanthemums
and then climbed the lilac tree. He felt unsettled
and grumpy and sad.

"I hate changes!" said Mac.

12. Mac Runs Away

Mac had decided that he would run away the day before Alice and Fred left. Perhaps they would change their minds. Perhaps they would decide to stay!

Jenny and Bronwen travelled up from their homes in the south of England to help with all the clearing out that had to be done. Deep down everyone knew that Alice and Fred were determined to buy a house further south and so Number Five had to be ready for sale when the time came. Jenny and Bronwen were great organizers. Everything was put into three piles:

* Things that Alice and Fred wanted for the new house.
* Things that the grown-up children wanted for themselves.
* Things to be recycled or given away or thrown out.

Jenny and Bronwen were fast workers and in no time at all, they emptied cupboards and wardrobes. They turned out drawers and stacked up rubbish. Sacks of things were taken to charity shops or the rubbish tip. They packed some childhood toys and books for themselves. They arranged for some of the furniture to be sold and some to be put into storage. It was all very efficient, but the house soon looked old and tired and unloved. Finally they organized a firm to come after they had left and clean the house from top to bottom. They hugged their parents.

"Goodbye Mum. Goodbye Dad. See you next week when you stay with us. It's sad to say goodbye to this old house." And they drove away in Jenny's smart car.

The cleaners came with brushes and mops and vacuum cleaners. Mac hated that. He disappeared outside and watched from the kitchen window sill, anxious to see what was happening to his house. Soon the house looked clean and bare and empty. Mac watched dust sheets being put over the remaining furniture.

He knew very well when Alice and Fred were almost ready to leave. He watched the suitcases stacked in the hall ready to go into the car. He saw his basket and bowl and dish being taken next door. He saw Alice clearing out the fridge. He realized that the next day they would leave. He ate a hearty amount of food that night and then slipped away for a lovely nocturnal prowl. He planned to stay away for at least two nights. He wanted people to be really worried!

After a rainy September, October was a month of shining golden sunlit days. Mac decided to visit the Water of Leith where there was so much to see. The water level was high and he enjoyed watching the swirling water from the safe distance of a high tree. The bluebells were long finished and the wild garlic had gone. But there were sharp autumn smells of bonfires. Brambles were heavy on branches and the fallen leaves lay crisp and crunchy on the paths. The elderberries were still darkly purple. There were lots of birds that were different from the garden birds. There were ducks and swans and herons. Once he saw a dipper. Sometimes he could see the brilliant flash of a kingfisher.

There were bridges to cross and steps to explore. In the daytime, cyclists whizzed past ringing their bells importantly. Children came after school and played. Many people walked their dogs by the river. Mac did not like dogs but he knew that at night-time he was safe. However, at night there was the much more dangerous smell of foxes and he had to move with care. He felt the thrill of exploration within him again during those early autumn nights. The first day he managed without eating. On the second day he was very hungry. Luckily he found a newspaper that had been wrapped around fish and chips, and he was glad to eat the greasy remains. But he slept badly that night. There were owls crying mournfully and two foxes scavenged for food.

"I shall go back tomorrow and see what has happened," he decided.

By the time he arrived back at the garden of Number Five, he knew that Alice and Fred had left. So they had not been worried enough to stay and look for him.

"They didn't care enough," he thought. "I want to have a family who cares enough." Deep down he was sad that they had not come looking for him. "I want a family who will love me enough to look for me until they find me," he said to himself. He felt hurt and lonely. He flicked his tail and made plans.

He decided to stay away for one more night. Then he would make an entrance that everyone would remember.

13. Making An Entrance

When dawn broke the next day, Mac was tired and very hungry. He had not given himself a good wash for two days and he felt very out of sorts. He needed food and attention and a comfy bed. Most of all he wanted people to love him. Alice and Fred had gone from Number Five. Now he must go back to the Musical Doctors and see if they cared enough. He would visit them and the neighbourhood in a way that they would never forget. He waited until late in the afternoon before beginning the journey home.

Although he usually visited the two doctors by the back garden, he cautiously made his way across two busy roads, round the whole block of houses, padded along the pavement and walked up the front path of Number Seven. With a quick leap he jumped to the window sill of the front bay window of the room downstairs. He looked in to the downstairs room from outside. This was the room that had the big table, the grand piano, the music stands and piles of sheet music. It was quite interesting to look at things from the outside in. And then he saw that there were people in the room concentrating on the music.

"Good!" he thought. "This will give them music!" He made himself comfortable and gave himself a quick lick. Then he opened his mouth.

He howled as loudly as he knew how. He howled and he growled. He yelled and he screeched. He stopped only for long enough to make sure that people were listening and then he started again.

Dr Helen and Dr Emily were coaching three children for a concert. One was playing the cello, and two of them were playing violins. When they heard the terrible noise at the front window, everyone stopped playing.

"Oh Mac, dear Mac!" said Dr Emily, as she ran to open the front door, "I am so glad you have come home."

Dr Helen went to the fridge and brought out the saucer of minced liver that she had prepared. She too abandoned her music teaching to entice Mac into the house.

"Mac," she wheedled, "see what we have for you. Lovely liver. Do come in."

Mac was hungry and the food smelt delicious. Besides, he was not cross with them. He just felt he had to make a fuss so that people knew that his feelings had been hurt by Alice and Fred leaving.

He climbed down from the window sill and walked in through the front door of Number Seven. First he walked into the kitchen and circled it carefully. Then he ate the liver and drank some milk. Then he found the room where the startled children had been left.

"Did all that noise come from a cat?" one of them asked in wonder. "I think he made more noise than I did when I was starting to learn the violin." And they all stared in awe at the beautiful cat who had made such a loud screeching noise.

"Well," said Dr Helen, "He has had a shock today. He was lost."

"Lost?" said Mac. "Lost? I was no such thing."

And to show that his feelings were still very ruffled, he jumped up onto the table and carefully pawed the pile of sheet music so that it trembled like a jelly and then slid in slow motion to the floor. Then he sat down on the next pile of music and he washed himself very carefully all over. He washed his paws and then his face and his head. He washed over his right shoulder and then over his left shoulder. He lay on his back and washed his tummy. He sat on his left side and put his right hind leg in the air and licked hard. Then he sat on his right side and put his left hind leg in the air. He spread out his claws on each paw and licked and tugged and groomed. There was not a square inch of him that he did not clean with great thoroughness.

The doctors and their pupils watched helplessly as Mac completed his toilet. Then Mac sat up straight and tall, jumped onto the most comfortable chair in the room and curled himself into a very tight ball with his tail covering his eyes.

"I think that is the lesson over for today," said Dr Helen to the children. "I am sure you will all play really well at the concert. Let's go and find some biscuits." And she led the way to the kitchen.

As soon as Dr Helen had led the children into the kitchen, Mac, who had not yet gone to sleep, opened his eyes and jumped down. He walked upstairs to the big drawing room. Good. There was a fire in the hearth and the room was warm. He liked this room best. But still he had not finished. He went into every room and examined it, rubbing his neck against the door, scratching the carpets with his claws, making sure that his own Mac scent was all over the house. This was his house and no one would turn him out. Only then did he go back to the drawing room, jump onto the big soft chair with the cushions of faded gold silk and fall deeply asleep.

14. Fights and a Fall

Dr Emily and Dr Helen were devoted to Mac. And after that first day, Mac fitted into the house very well. He played in the garden when the music lessons were on. And when the nasty old gardener came, he went back to the silent overgrown garden at Number Five. After the children had gone home he really enjoyed listening to Dr Helen playing the cello. He sat close to her in the evening and when she played his favourites, Mac would lift up his head and purr.

"So," she would say, "You really *do* like Bach best, you clever cat."

A few months later, Helen and Emily received a letter from Alice and Fred. They had found a lovely small house in the south of England. It was just what they wanted and was close to two of their children. Number Five was to be sold. The only problem was Mac. Would Helen and Emily take him for good?

Of course Helen and Emily agreed. And so it was arranged. Mac liked the Musical Doctors and he loved the house and garden.

As time passed, Mac began to feel well and truly settled. He liked to appear soft and gentle at home, but at night, when he slipped through the open window of the scullery and patrolled the neighbourhood, he was a different cat. He kept all the other cats in order and had some notable fights. These belonged to the secret life that cats have. But one day he could not disguise a very sore back leg. When he came home, he limped and left a trail of blood.

"Oh Emily," cried Helen, "Poor Mac is hurt. We shall have to take him to the vet." By this time the vet knew Mac quite well.

"Had another fight then?" he grinned. He examined the leg. "Looks like he's taken on a dog this time. I tell you, that cat is the terror of the neighbourhood. I'll stitch him up and we'll see how it goes. Try to keep him in at night."

"But Doctor," said Helen, "he is the gentlest of animals. He never goes out at night and he is such a sweet cat."

"Most cats have a secret life," said the vet. "I've lost count of the cats I have attended to in this area. Some one must be inflicting the scars. Mark my words he's the top cat around here!" And he stroked Mac and winked at him. He guessed that Mac was showing who was boss to all concerned, humans and cats. "You're a handsome fellow," he said, "and a great warrior."

Just as Mac thought that things were settling down nicely, something happened that changed everything.

Dr Emily was walking downstairs carrying a large pile of music in one hand and her fiddle in the other. Suddenly she was falling down the stairs. The fiddle fell with a crash. The music fluttered through the air like autumn leaves, and Dr Emily lay very still and quiet at the foot of the stairs and then she started to groan.

"I do believe I've broken something. I am so sore," she gasped. Quickly Dr Helen telephoned for the doctor. Soon the doctor arrived and then an ambulance.

The doctor shook her head. "I have warned you about this," she said. "The two of you should have moved to a smaller place ages ago. This is far too big for you at your age." Then she gave Dr Helen a big hug because she liked them both so much. "Every cloud has a silver lining," she said. "Maybe this will be the beginning of something good for you both." Dr Emily was taken to hospital where her broken hip was replaced and she eventually learned to walk again.

"I have to learn to climb as well as walk," she told the physiotherapist. "There are fifty-four steps in our house."

"Fifty-four steps in the house!" said the physiotherapist in horror, and told the nurse.

"Fifty-four steps in the house!" said the nurse in horror, and told the social worker.

"Fifty-four steps in the house!" said the social worker in horror, and told the occupational therapist.

"Fifty-four steps in the house!" said the occupational therapist in horror, and told the consultant.

"Fifty-four steps in the house!" said the consultant and laughed. "That's why she's such a tough old bird; over eighty years old and still making such beautiful music. She's promised to come and play for the Christmas concert if we get her walking. And we shall. We shall." And the consultant grinned. She was one of his favourite patients because she had such spirit.

However the consultant and the physiotherapist and the nurse and the social worker and the occupational therapist all agreed on one thing.

"She can't go on living there. We shall have to speak to her sister." So the consultant and the physiotherapist and the nurse and the social worker and the occupational therapist all met together with Dr Helen and explained that although Dr Emily would be able to walk again, they would have to find another house. "Besides," said the consultant and the physiotherapist and the social worker and the nurse and the occupational therapist, "you are both over eighty years old. You deserve a quieter life now."

The consultant, who liked to play the piano himself when he had a moment, knew what a big thing the musical doctors were being asked to do. "You can still play in chamber orchestras. You can still give recitals. You can still do charity work. You will be able to find a flat big enough for an upright piano. Just don't go back to such a huge house at your age."

So Dr Helen and Dr Emily knew that their lives would have to change. But what about Mac?

15. A Job Lot

The two sisters came to the sensible decision that they would have to sell the house and move to a more convenient place. They found exactly what they were looking for. It was a big new building in the same area with lots of flats for older people. There were lifts as well as stairs and there was a warden who would help to look after them. There was a large dining room and it was possible to have a good hot meal in the middle of the day. That suited them both, because they were too old and tired to bake or cook for themselves now. But no pets were allowed. Not even Mac.

Dr Helen came home from visiting Dr Emily in hospital.

"Oh Mac," she said, "What am I to do about you? We cannot take you with us. What shall I do?"

Mac knew that Dr Helen was worried. He rubbed against her ankles. "You still have me," he said to her, "I shall look after you."

"Oh Mac, dear Mac," she said, "I shall have to sell the house to someone who likes cats and does not have a dog." She packed all her music in boxes and talked out loud, partly to herself and partly to Mac. "Alice and Fred are in England for good now. They will never be back. I wonder if Bronwen would take you? But she is acting now and is always on tour. I don't even know how to get in touch with her. I wonder if any of the children who have been my pupils would take you? I shall have to give you to someone who would look after you."

"Nobody will give me away," said Mac to himself. "I shall decide."

Mac did not like seeing boxes brought into the house and packed. He knew it meant change. He knew it meant trouble.

"Why does everyone have to leave?" he thought to himself. "It was just perfect. There is good food and there are comfortable chairs and if the music is good I listen and if it is noisy I go into the garden. Why do we have to change? It is all perfectly horrid."

Dr Helen's solicitor came to the house and arranged that it should go up for sale. He sent a firm to pack the books and he arranged for the music to be given away to the music unit of the school where she worked. He helped her to make decisions about what to keep and what to give away. He arranged for a firm to come and clean the big old dusty house. He was very efficient.

He sat in the upstairs drawing room and sipped tea.

"Everything is ready now. Emily is doing well and is ready to move. You are ready to move. People will start to come and view the house soon. Then you can enjoy a happy retirement."

"But there is Mac," wailed Dr Helen, "I have to sell the house to someone who will take Mac."

The tall friendly solicitor stroked his beard. "I think we could arrange for Mac to go to a cattery, if necessary." He looked at Mac doubtfully, then he smiled. "He certainly is the handsomest cat I have ever seen. Let's hope someone comes to view the house who likes cats. We can sell them together. A job lot!" And he tickled Mac under his chin.

Mac moved away with dignity. Then opened his mouth and snarled. "I am not to be sold," he said to himself and swept out of the room.

The solicitor looked at the retreating back and erect tail.

"On second thoughts," he said thoughtfully, "I wouldn't be surprised if that cat sold the house himself. Did you ever see such a look as he gave me? You would almost think he could understand every word I said."

"Of course he understands," said Dr Helen. "Of course he understands. He would not like a dog living here. He does not like noisy music. He likes classical music. The house has to go to someone who likes classical music."

"Oh," said the solicitor, wondering if he had heard aright. "I see. And does he have a favourite composer?"

"He likes Bach. Especially the cello suites. But anything of Bach he enjoys."

"Bach," repeated the solicitor, who preferred a bit of jazz himself. "I see."

"He likes Mozart too," added Dr Helen in encouragement, "but there is no doubt that he responds best to Bach."

"And does he have any other preferences?" the solicitor asked faintly.

"He likes oily fish better than white fish — mackerel, salmon, trout — that sort of thing. He really enjoys a tin of evaporated milk but the vet says not to give him too much so he only has it on Sundays as a treat.

"Well," said the solicitor, "I'll prepare the advertisement and we shall see how the sale goes." And he took leave of Dr Helen. He wondered as he thundered down the stairs whether she had been pulling his leg. But as he passed the large practice room on the ground floor he heard cello music playing on the CD player and Mac was listening with his nose in the air, purring in delight.

"Barmy," he said, as he let himself out.

16. Sold!

Many people, many, *many* people came to look at the house. There were tall people and short people. There were people with children. There were people with grannies. There were English people and Scottish people. There were Indian families and American families. Some had dogs. Some had cats. Some had cats and dogs.

Some of them refused to take a cat and went away. Some were so anxious to buy the house that they would have promised anything. But when they were introduced to Mac, he always knew that they were not sincere and he walked out of the room, his tail held high.

"What shall I do?" worried Dr Helen. She was becoming tired and tearful as she showed people round the house where she and her sister had spent so many happy years. People thought that the house was old fashioned and required modernization. They planned to tear things apart and 'do it up.'

Or worse, a businessman came around and decided he could separate it into two or even three flats.

"Could make my fortune on this one," he thought to himself.

Dr Helen loved the house and did not like people to call it shabby or quaint. She did not like to hear them murmur, "It would cost a fortune to do up." She became sad that no one wanted the large old house with the beautiful garden. "Why can they not see how lovely it is?" she thought. "Why can they not feel the happiness and hear the music and love the garden? I shall have to speak to my solicitor and tell him to stop the people coming."

Then the jolly consultant who had looked after Dr Emily telephoned.

"I have friends in Sussex who are moving to Edinburgh. They can't find a house big enough. Peter is going to work at the University. They don't mind an old fashioned house. Would you let them see it?"

So the last person who was allowed to see the house was Marion, who had travelled by train from Brighton to London and then overnight from London to Edinburgh. Old Dr Helen met her at the front door.

"Do you have a dog?" asked old Dr Helen.

"We don't have any dogs," smiled Marion, "just two children."

"Do you like cats?" asked old Dr Helen.

"I love cats," said Marion in surprise. "How did you know?"

So old Dr Helen showed Marion the house from top to bottom.

"It's beautiful," thought Marion. "I love the old fashioned ribbed brass door handles. I love the high ceilings and the beautiful cornices. The garden is perfect. The snowdrops must have been wonderful, the daffodils are beautiful and although it is only March, you can see the tulips pushing up. I wonder what else there is in this magic garden. I love it. I hope it won't cost too much."

Last of all Dr Helen took Marion into the drawing room to introduce her to Mac. He sat on the table by the bay window, with his back straight and stiff and still. He would not turn his head.

"What a gorgeous cat," said Marion.

"If you buy the house," said old Dr Helen, "will you take Mac too?"

Mac lashed his tail.

"No one gives me away," he said, "I will decide."

"Well," said Marion, "the big question is, if we buy the house, would Mac take us?"

They sat down, old Dr Helen and Marion, and began to drink their coffee. And Mac turned to look at this wise woman. Perhaps he would let her live in his house after all. He jumped off the table and walked towards her, his tail high in the air, his whiskers bristling, and he stared hard.

"Please like me," thought Marion, "I really like this house."

She stretched out her hand towards Mac. When Mac sniffed her hand he smelt kindness. He sat at her feet, they looked at each other and Mac purred quietly. In that moment they became friends. In that moment the house became hers.

"I have decided," thought Mac.

That evening many phone calls were made.

Dr Helen phoned her solicitor and told him she had sold her house to someone who liked cats.

"Good work," said the solicitor, and poured himself a large *Lagavulin*.

Dr Helen phoned Emily's consultant and told him that she had sold the house to his friends from Sussex.

"Jolly good show," said the consultant. "By the way, did she tell you she was crazy about cats?"

Marion phoned her family before catching the night train back to Sussex and told them about the lovely new house.

"Will there be room for all my books?" asked her husband, Peter.

"Is there enough room to play football in the garden?" asked her son, Donald.

"Are you coming home soon?" asked her daughter, Catriona.

"Yes to all three questions," said Marion. "And guess what? The house comes with a beautiful intelligent tabby cat called Mac."

"Well ... as long as he stays in the kitchen," said Peter.

"Do you think he would learn to kick a ball?" asked Donald.

"Can he sleep on my bed?" asked Catriona.

17. Moving Day

It was a lovely sunny day when the new family arrived. Mac hid under the laurel bush in the front garden and watched. There were two large removal vans. The men unloaded beds and wardrobes, tables and chairs, desks and a piano, armchairs and sofas, bookcases and more bookcases. Then boxes, and boxes, and boxes of books. There were ninety-nine crates of books.

"I hope there's room for me," thought Mac anxiously.

Peter went into the upstairs drawing room where Mac used to sit by the window. It was now Peter's study and he began to unpack his books.

Marion went into the kitchen and began to unpack her survival bag. It contained an electric kettle and lots of mugs. There were packets of tea and coffee and sugar, a carton of milk, a box of biscuits, orange squash and a large fruitcake. It had some cat food, aspirins, tissues, a note pad and pen, a good book and a large slab of chocolate.

"I'm glad I kept these with me," she thought, "I wonder where Mac is?" She went to the back door, and called his name, then returned to the kitchen and started unpacking.

Catriona, who was nine, had two long thick fair pigtails. She ran around the house, upstairs and downstairs looking into every room.

"I can't find him," she wailed.

Donald was eleven and felt very grown-up because he was going to high school after the summer holidays. He ran upstairs to the top floor to the room furthest away from everyone else.

"I want this room," he shouted. "Bags I have this room."

Marion directed where the furniture should go. All the furniture with a red label went downstairs. Everything with a blue label went to the first floor. Everything with a green label went to the top floor. Each door had a number on it and the labels, as well as being coloured also had a number. The removal men were very glad that the piano had a red label and stayed downstairs. All the time this was happening, Marion and Catriona kept looking for Mac. They opened the walk-in cupboards and the funny flat Scottish shelved cupboards in every room called a 'press.' They looked in the cupboard under the stairs and in the linen cupboard upstairs.

"He's gone," sobbed Catriona, "he's decided he doesn't like us."

"Nonsense," said Marion. "No self-respecting cat would come near this house at the moment. Both doors wide open. Children shouting and running all over the place. Men going up and down the stairs with big heavy loads. Time for elevenses. Everyone deserves it. Come and help me."

So Marion and Catriona made tea and poured squash. They opened a packet of biscuits and cut the fruitcake and called for everyone to come. It was good to sit in the back garden and have a long cool drink followed by a mug of tea.

Everyone worked hard. At four o'clock the removal men called it a day.

"Thanks for the tea and stuff, love," they said in Sussex accents that were already beginning to sound out-of-place. "We'll be back at half past eight tomorrow. Another three or four hours should see it done."

Marion opened the case with all the sheets and pillowslips. She and Peter made up the old beds in the new house. Suddenly the new rooms appeared friendly and familiar as the children saw their favourite duvet covers and their books and the well-loved old toys. Donald had a favourite football and an old green rabbit that always had to be stitched because the stuffing kept leaking. Catriona had a lot of dolls and a large family of koalas.

At seven o'clock, Marion straightened her back and smoothed the last bed cover. "That's it. Let's go and stretch our legs and find some food." Peter and Marion and the children walked down the road, turned the corner onto the main road and found a great fish and chip shop. Peter had haggis and chips. Donald had fried spring roll in batter and chips. Catriona and Marion both chose something that they thought might tempt Mac: Catriona had chicken and chips and Marion chose fish and chips. They put out half the chicken and half the fish at the back door with a saucer of water and a saucer of milk.

Later that evening, when it was nearly dark and everyone else was in bed, Marion went out to the garden. She walked down to the two tall trees at

the bottom of the garden. "We have an ash tree
and a lilac tree," she said. "How lucky we are to
have found such a lovely house and to have such a
beautiful garden. I hope Mac finds us. And I hope
we can all be happy together." Then slowly she
walked back into the house, enjoying the cool summer evening smells. She did not see the long dark
form lying flat on the lilac tree branch, or see the
eyes silently watching.

But in the morning, the fish and the chicken had
gone.

18. Home Coming

Gradually during that long warm summer, the new family settled in. Peter finally unpacked all his books and started to prepare his classes for the new session. Donald and Catriona explored the house and the garden and the area round about. They were lonely without the old friends they had had in Sussex. Marion rearranged the furniture and made some curtains. She was happy wandering in the garden and exploring Edinburgh, where she had lived when she was a girl. She took the children to buy uniforms for their new schools. Catriona had a pink blouse, a brown pinafore, a brown cardigan and a brown blazer with a pink badge. Donald had a navy blue blazer, a white shirt, a school tie and long grey trousers. He felt very tall and grown-up.

All this time, Mac glided like a shadow at the bottom of the garden in the long summer evenings. Sometimes Marion would see him in the distance but as soon as she opened the back door he disappeared. Every evening Marion put out fresh cat food for him and a bowl of water. Every morning the dishes were empty.

"Probably a hedgehog," said Peter, teasing her.

But Marion knew better. Sometimes she went alone into the garden just before midnight.

"Mac, please come home," she whispered. And in the scented stillness of the garden, she felt the presence of Mac.

During those summer days, Peter and Marion

took Donald and Catriona to the zoo and to the botanic gardens. They visited Edinburgh Castle and the palace of Holyrood House and the Chamber Street Museums. They made themselves dizzy climbing round and round and round the spiral stairway to the top of the Scott Monument. They walked to the top of Blackford Hill on the south side of Edinburgh. They walked up past Swanston to the T-woods. One day they scrambled to the top of Arthur's Seat and looked over the Firth of Forth to Fife. Peter and Marion had worked in India where the children were born and then in England. In both places they had been really happy. But as they saw Edinburgh spread out before them and beyond the Firth of Forth, the hills of the north, they looked at each other and smiled.

"We have come home," they said. "It's good to come home."

They clambered down Arthur's Seat and took the bus home. Peter went straight to his study to work. The children ran into the living room and switched on the television set. Marion went into the kitchen to set out ham and salad for tea. As she opened the door, she saw Mac sitting outside the kitchen window. Very gently Marion opened the back door and propped it open so that he could make his escape if he wanted to. Slowly he walked all around the kitchen, sniffing the new cooker, the new kitchen units and the new linoleum. His ears were flat against his head and his whiskers twitched as he took in the changes and the similarities. He looked longingly at the old rocking chair beside the fireplace.

Just then Donald flung open the kitchen door.

"When's tea?" he shouted. "I want to go to the park and play football."

Mac was out of the house quicker than a streak of lightning.

As they sat at tea together, Marion told them about Mac.

"A figment of your imagination," teased Peter.

"I didn't see him," said Donald grumpily.

"I wish I'd been there," said Catriona sadly.

"He'll be back," said Marion. "Let's go out and play in the park before bedtime." And they did.

The next day as they were clearing away the breakfast dishes, Mac came to the window again.

"Don't move a muscle," said Marion, "And don't talk. Just freeze." Again Marion opened the back door and propped it open. Again Mac cautiously entered the kitchen. He looked at the four people standing as still as statues. Very deliberately he walked past them, through the hall and upstairs.

"It is my house," thought Mac. "I shall have to show them. I am not going to be pushed around any more. I shall have to show them who is boss."

He padded upstairs and nosed open the door of the drawing room, which was now Peter's study.

"Hang on," said Peter, "I thought he was going to stay downstairs in the kitchen? I don't think I want him in My Study."

The four humans tiptoed upstairs and into the study to see the cat that had sold them the house. He was on Peter's desk by the window, sitting straight and tall with his tail curled neatly around his front paws. His ears were pricked forward and his long white whiskers quivered with delight and excitement.

"You know," began Peter, "I do think the cat should be kept downstairs in the kitchen."

"Dad," both the children said, "don't be mean."

"I don't think," said Peter again, "that I want him in My Study."

"Too late," smiled Marion.

"I have come home," said Mac.

19. Mac the Mighty Hunter

Before the new family moved in, a new kitchen had been installed. But after they were in the house, they realized that more had to be done. Dr Helen had assured Marion that the house was "completely modernized."

"We have gas," she had explained. "And electricity was put in when I was a girl, so nothing requires to be done." And she had smiled encouragingly.

But a long time had passed since Dr Helen had been a girl and Marion felt that a great deal more did have to be done. She loved the old shutters that would keep the house cosy in wintertime. She liked the faded velvet carpet on the fifty-four stairs and the old-fashioned brass stair rods. "But we can't live in the past," she said to Peter, "especially as we shall probably have Grandpa and Great Auntie staying with us from time to time."

One thing led to another and finally plans were made to replace the two bathrooms, to put in central heating and to make a guest bedroom suitable for Grandpa. On the top floor, the old bath, which had not been used for years, had rusted away under the enamel and came down the stairs in two sacks. So the plumbers came, and the electricians and the joiners and the plasterers. Last of all the decorators came and then the carpet layers.

When the men lifted the floorboards up, Mac loved to jump in and explore underneath each room. Such exciting smells there were, wild dangerous smells! These were not cooking smells or Christmas smells or farmyard smells or garden smells. These were living smells. These were mouse smells!

"Mac, come out of there," Marion would say. And to the workmen as she brought them cups of tea or mugs of soup, "Do keep an eye on him, please. I can't bear to think of him getting trapped underneath."

"Don't you worry, love," they said, "he can look after himself. He's a sharp one that. Any more of that chocolate cake?"

Mac wondered if Marion knew about the mice. Could she not smell them there? Perhaps she liked them. She appeared to be unconcerned and went about the house unpacking boxes and tidying cupboards. She sang a lot and talked to Mac often. Mac loved it when he went into a room and Marion stopped what she was doing and came over to tickle him under the chin. Sometimes she would sit on the nearest chair amid the packing cases and Mac would jump on her knee.

"What a sensible woman," thought Mac. "This is what a cat's life should be, a warm lap, a good tickle under the chin and time for a snooze."

Several times he tried to tell her about the mice but she went on stroking his head and cuddling him.

"I'll take care of the mice for you," vowed Mac. "I don't want you to be bothered by them."

Sure enough, when the last floorboard was down, the last room painted and the last carpet laid, the mice began to squeeze through the tiniest holes and came out at night to play.

One night when the children were in bed asleep and Peter was away at a conference, Marion made a mug of cocoa and sat by the fire.

"I must go to bed," she said to Mac, "but I am so tired, I haven't the energy to move." She sat back in the armchair, quietly, quietly, and closed her eyes. "Why won't you climb on my knee, Mac?" she asked. He would not budge and she was too tired to persuade him.

Mac crouched at her feet, as still and silent as she was, but with eyes open, brain alert, vigilant. Suddenly, he shot like an arrow across the room. He pounced and swooped in one graceful movement. It happened quickly and quietly, but when he padded back to Marion, Mac carried a mouse, its neck cleanly and swiftly snapped. Mac looked at Marion with his intelligent eyes and dropped the dead mouse at her feet. He would know very soon if this had been a good move.

"Mac!" she cried. "You clever cat. I didn't even know that we had a mouse. I hope there aren't any more. If there are, you can catch them for me. I don't mind field mice in the fields, but I do not like mice in the house. Well done you. Now I am awake enough to climb the stairs and go to bed."

So she did.

"A mouse," said Mac to himself. "A mouse — as if there is ever only one single mouse in a house. If she only knew." He watched her go and crouched down to keep watch. "Now I know what to do to help her," he said to himself.

In the morning there were three dead mice lying neatly at the bottom of the stairs. For over three weeks Mac hunted and killed all the mice in the house for Marion.

"He smote them hip and thigh," murmured Marion, who liked quotations when they fitted the situation. Each day there were more and at the end of a month the tally was twenty-nine.

"Mac," said Marion, "you are earning your keep. Thank you."

20. Mac's Chosen Family

Mac had spent all his life adapting to other people and trying to be loved. He was wary of this new family to begin with. What if they were difficult to live with? What if they changed their minds about wanting him? After all, *he* had sold the house to Marion. He decided that he had to train them well *right from the start*.

Peter could have been a problem. So Mac knew that he must make it clear that he, Mac, had sold them the house. They were allowed to live in it provided they respected his needs. He knew that if he could get into the front drawing room — now Peter's study — he would have made his point. In the event, it turned out to be easy. Peter was really a big softie inside. When faced with the reality of a handsome cat sitting on top of the desk, he gave in. In fact, he surrendered completely. He learned to work around Mac's place on the top left hand corner of the desk and meekly moved his books and papers when they encroached on Mac's space.

Catriona adored Mac from the beginning. When she came home from school she always searched the house and garden to find Mac. She had a piercing whistle which Mac soon recognized.

"That's my girl," he said to himself, "that's my girl calling for me."

And he would fly through gardens and along walls and bound up the garden to greet her. When she picked him up to give him a cuddle, he climbed

onto her shoulder and draped himself around
her neck while she walked carefully back to the
house.

Catriona wanted Mac to sleep in her bedroom.
To Mac's relief, Marion was firm about this. Mac
was given a free run of the kitchen and scullery
at night, but the kitchen door was closed. Mac
preferred it this way. It meant that after the
household was asleep, he could patrol the mouse
runs and when he was satisfied that there were
no mice there, he slipped out of the open window, and through the old iron bars which had
been placed there to deter burglars. Then he was
master, not only of the garden at Number Seven,
but also of many gardens in the area. Only where
there were dogs did he hesitate, and only then if
they and he had not yet reached an agreement.
Otherwise he was King of his patch and Lord of
the manor.

Catriona, like Dr Helen's pupils, was very musical; she played the recorder and the clarinet. The
early years with the clarinet were difficult. Marion
could hear the loud discordant noises from downstairs and she gently closed the kitchen door.

"I can't stand that," she thought, "it'll give me
a headache."

Catriona found it hard to make the right note.
When it became too terrible, Mac put his nose in
the air and started to howl.

"This is dreadful, dreadful, dreadful. Why can't
she play the cello?"

Sometimes the noises were so bad that he dived
under the bed. But she practised long and hard

over the years. She played in a concert band at school and a jazz band and by the time she was playing Mozart's clarinet quintet, Mac was very pleased with her.

"I knew she could do it if she kept at it," he said. "Thank goodness she got better."

But still he missed the cello.

Donald pretended that Mac meant nothing to him, but secretly he loved Mac and would play games with him when no one was looking. Often a solemn faced boy and a mesmerized cat were to be seen flicking ping-pong balls backwards and forwards to each other.

School friends bothered Mac to begin with. He was quite alarmed when several young girls would scramble upstairs to Catriona's bedroom on the top floor. He was even more alarmed when large numbers of young teenage boys arrived home at four o'clock, settled into the kitchen and raided all the cake and biscuit tins. It was then that he found refuge with Grandpa.

Grandpa lived with the family occasionally and when he wasn't staying with them, he lived over the road. Wherever he was living, he spent every afternoon in the sitting room downstairs. He loved it when the children came home from school. He liked it when they came in and said, "Hello Grandpa, how are you today?" and kissed him on his bristly old cheek. Then they disappeared to the kitchen for noisy happy times with their friends, and Marion and Mac came into the front room with tea and scones or a cake. Mac liked Grandpa. In cat years, they were not far apart in age and each respected the other's need for sleep and sustenance and quiet.

Sometimes Mac would sit on Grandpa's lap and purr. While Grandpa went over some of the finer points of his time in North Africa during the Second World War, Mac would dream his own dreams. Then he would jump down and stretch in front of the fire.

Life with this family was very different from the quiet life he had known before, where Fred had been out and Alice had painted. It was even more unlike the quiet musical life with Dr Helen and Dr Emily. But he discovered that he liked it. He liked it very much indeed.

For one thing, when the front door banged for the last time each morning, he knew that Marion and he were alone in the house. She usually cleared away the breakfast things and then settled down with a mug of coffee on the old rocking chair beside the gas fire in the kitchen. Mac often jumped onto her knee and they rocked together in companionable silence.

Sometimes Marion would say things like, "Mac is my gentle lovely puss cat. He is 'a verray parfit gentil knight'." She was given to quoting things no one else understood, but Mac always knew what she meant. They understood each other perfectly.

"What a sensible woman she is," Mac often thought to himself, "very sensible indeed." Unlike Dr Helen and Dr Emily, she loved gardening and spent a lot of time weeding and hoeing and planning for the next year. She wanted to plant lots of bulbs but decided to wait until the first spring to find out what was planted there already. Meantime, she enjoyed making plans. Mac loved to feel that she was planning for a long stay.

"Good," he thought. "They are planning to stay for ever."

Sometimes Marion went out but she worked at home too. Then her study would be cosy and filled with gentle music from her CD player. She had bought a set of discs of Bach's cello suites especially for Mac and together they played them over and over and over again. Then he would sleep, in the garden or in the house. What happy dreams he had in those days. Life was good.

By the time he had had a good sleep, the children were back like a whirlwind. He could choose to play if he wanted to or he could join Grandpa or Marion. Then Marion prepared the evening meal. That was good too because she always gave him little bits to nibble if there was something interesting being cooked. In the evenings he visited Peter in his study.

"I have trained this family *very* well," he said to himself.

Christmas turned out to be even more exciting than with Fred and Alice. They put up a large tree in the window. He knew now that it was not for climbing but he did enjoy helping with the paper chains. The smells were just as good and the dinner on Christmas Day was even better. There were always students from overseas who came to visit and they took many photographs. Mac sat as still as a statue and gave a left profile then a right profile. He sometimes stared very hard at the camera and sometimes he closed his eyes just as the flash came. He enjoyed it when they went away — lots of turkey scraps and plates to lick clean.

"This is life," thought Mac. "Nothing to worry about now. They are not going to retire or fall down stairs or move house. Everything is just fine. I have trained this family well. I shall let them stay in my house. And *I* shall stay here forever."

21. Ends and Beginnings

And so the years passed. The house was full of children and the smells of home baking and cooking. It was filled with music and laughter. There were books piled high in all the rooms and sometimes on the stairs. The garden was wild enough. The house was warm enough. Mac purred often and said to himself, "I made a good decision." Everyone in the neighbourhood knew Mac. He had lived so long that he was the oldest cat around. He had been the best mouser, the fiercest fighter and had the loudest purr. People would stop Marion in the street and ask her,

"How is Mac? Is he still alive? He must be very old now."

The children went off to college and to see the world. Mac thought that was good too. He liked a quieter life now. He was able to be with Marion a lot of the time.

Sometimes they were in the garden together. When she was weeding, he stayed close, so that she could stretch out her hand and tickle him behind the ears. If she worked in the shade, he walked to the nearest place in the sun and stretched out to feel the heat in his old bones. He did not like it when she brought out the lawn mower. Then he climbed the lilac tree to be away from the noise and the spraying grass. He liked the end of gardening best. Then she cleaned the tools, put them away in the shed and came out with a mug of tea.

She sat on the old wooden bench faded silvery grey
with the sun and he would stretch out beside her.
Together they admired the clematis and the lupins
or they closed their eyes and enjoyed the scent of
honeysuckle and roses.

Sometimes they were indoors together. Often
Marion would sit in the big old armchair and Mac
would sit on her knee, throbbing with joy. Even
when she had to work at her desk, there was a
space on the desk for Mac. She would scratch the
top of his head and say, "Come on, Mac. You are
my muse. Give me some inspiration today." And
he would purr with contentment while she typed
away. She played her CDs and thought of the gentle Helen and Emily.

If she had to be out of the house, Mac followed
the sun from room to room, finding a patch of
sunlight to sleep in. In the winter, he stayed by the
fire and dozed. In the summer he rolled in the catmint and dozed. Best of all, he scratched his claws
on the lilac tree and then lay along the broad low
branch and viewed the world.

"Marion loves me, myself, Mac," he thought,
"And I love her."

He was content.

One morning in early summer, Marion and
Peter saw that Mac looked dizzy. He fell over once
or twice and looked surprised each time. He drank
a lot of water. Then he staggered to the lilac tree.

"I feel too weak and wobbly to climb it today,"
said Mac. "Tomorrow I shall climb it. Today I shall
sleep below the gentle green leaves and the plumes
of purple flowers."

And he did.

He thought, "I am a happy cat."

And he fell asleep.

Marion found him asleep under the lilac tree that evening. She knew that he would not waken again.

"Lucky old puss," said the vet when he came. "I wish we could all die as sweetly."

Peter and Marion dug a big hole under the lilac tree for Mac. Catriona came home from Glasgow when she heard the news that Mac had died. Catriona put Mac into a linen pillowcase, very old and very thin, that had been embroidered by Marion's Grandma. Marion and Peter and Catriona picked some flowers from the garden — the last of the pheasant's eye narcissi, some bluebells, rosemary and some pink tulips. They laid Mac in the hole below the lilac tree, and covered him with the flowers they had picked.

"He was twenty-one and a half when he died," they said. "A good age."

They planted white wood anemones to mark his grave.

They wrote a letter to Donald that night. He was working in India and he did not hear the news for another week. He wandered around the bazaar in Guindy, Madras, and bought a little brass cat to take home.

But Marion missed Mac dreadfully with his great white whiskers and creamy bib, with his love of Bach and his friendly purr.

One day, a friend said, "Would you like a kitten? I know of a Norwegian Forest kitten looking for

a good home. He is a soft pale beige colour and very fluffy. He is eight weeks old and his name is Fudge."

Now Fudge the kitten plays beneath the lilac tree and sometimes when he catches a falling leaf or chases the butterflies, he feels a quiet presence watching over him. And sometimes he hears cello music in the distance. He is too young to know that he is listening to Bach. He rolls over and over in the catmint and then tries to climb the tree.

"I like it here," says Fudge, "I think I shall stay."

"He will decide," whispers Mac.

Glossary

Mixter-maxter — all mixed up

Fechter — the Scots word for fighter

Dunsyre Blue — a cheese made using the rich, unpasteurized milk of Ayrshire cattle

Lagavulin — a single malt Scotch whisky made on the island of Islay

Quotations

"When in doubt wash" comes from *Jennie* by Paul Gallico

"He smote them hip and thigh" comes from the Bible, Authorized Version, Judges 15:8

"a verray parfit gentil knight" comes from *The Canterbury Tales* by Geoffrey Chaucer

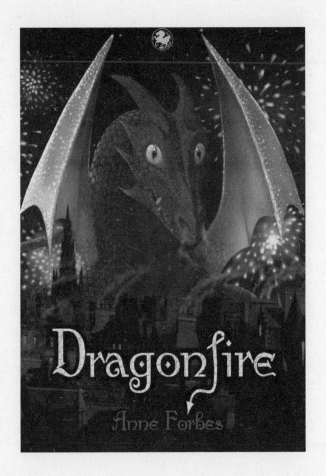

Dragonfire

Anne Forbes

Anne Forbes: *Dragonfire*

Clara and Neil have always known the MacArthurs, the little people who live under Arthur's Seat, in Holyrood Park, but they are not quite prepared for what else is living under the hill. Feuding faery lords, missing whisky, magic carpets, firestones and ancient spells ... where will it end? And how did it all start?

Set against the backdrop of the Edinburgh Fringe and Military Tattoo this is a fast-paced comic adventure, full of magic, mayhem and mystery ... and a dragon.

Alex Nye, *Chill*

Samuel is trapped by huge snowdrifts in an old, remote house. And that's not the only thing causing a cold shiver to creep down his spine. He feels like the ghostly figure in the locked library has a message ... but who is it for?

Fiona lives in the big house, but will that help the two of them to break the curse on her family? As the ice sets in, they uncover a deadly tale of betrayal and revenge.

Set on bleak Sheriffmuir near Stirling, this is a spooky tale of the past coming back to haunt the present.

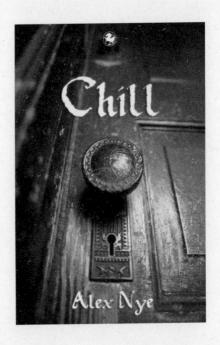

Contemporary Kelpies

Mike Nicholson, *Catscape*

Fergus can't believe it when his brand-new digital watch starts going backwards. Then he crashes (literally) into gadget-loving Murdo, and a second mystery comes to light — cats are going missing all over the neighbourhood. As the two boys start to investigate, they find help in some unexpected places.

Mike Nicholson won the Kelpies Prize with *Catscape*, his first novel, which is set in his home neighbourhood of Comely Bank, Edinburgh.

Contemporary Kelpies

Gill Arbuthnott, *Winterbringers*

St Andrews, Fife — not known for its glorious weather, but even so, Josh hadn't expected the sea to start to freeze and ice to creep up the beaches ... His summer holiday isn't looking too promising, especially as his only companions are a strange local girl, Callie, and her enormous dog, Luath.

Then they uncover the journal of an eighteenth-century girl who writes about a Kingdom of Summer, and suddenly find themselves thrown headlong into a storm of witches, ice creatures, magic and the Winter King. A permanent winter threatens unless they can help restore the natural balance of the seasons.

Can they stop the Winterbringers once and for all?

Contemporary Kelpies

Gill Arbuthnott, *The Chaos Clock*

Kate and David are eleven years old and best of friends, playing football and doing their museum project together. But in Edinburgh, where they live, time is coming unstuck and the past is breaking loose. Old Mr Flowerdew needs their help in the war between the Lords of Chaos and the Guardians of Time, centred around the mysterious Millennium Clock at the Royal Museum.

Can Kate use her grandmother's golden necklace to restrain the power of Chaos, and will David be able to help the Guardians, even if it means losing his mother all over again?

Contemporary Kelpies

Kathleen Fidler

The Desperate Journey

'A stirring tale of adventure, hardship and new
beginnings.' *Shelf Life*

Twins Kirsty and Davie Murray are forced to leave their
home and travel across Scotland to Glasgow. Not used to
city life, the family struggles to survive. The future looks
bleak as the children go to work in a cotton mill, where
they are in constant danger from machinery and the fore-
man's whip. Then the family are offered the chance to
join an emigrant ship bound for Hudson Bay in Canada,
and begin a perilous journey towards a new life in the Red
River Colony.

But will the Murrays survive the Atlantic crossing on a
disease-ridden ship? Even if they do, what will they find
in the strange new land?

Classic Kelpies

Kathleen Fidler

The Boy with the Bronze Axe

A classic story set in the ancient Stone Age village of Skara Brae on Orkney.

Kali and Brockan are in trouble. They have been using their stone axes to chip limpets off the rocks, but they've gone too far out and find themselves trapped by the tides. Then, an unexpected rescuer appears — a strange boy in a strange boat, carrying a strangely sharp axe of a type they have never seen before. Conflict arises as the village of Skara must decide what to do with the new ideas and practices that the boy brings. As a deadly storm threatens, the very survival of the village is in doubt.

The daily life, landscape and rituals of Skara are brought to life in striking, compelling detail. This is a fascinating and vividly portrayed story of life nearly 3,000 years ago.

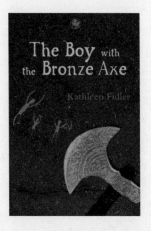

Classic Kelpies